Whose Eyes Are These?

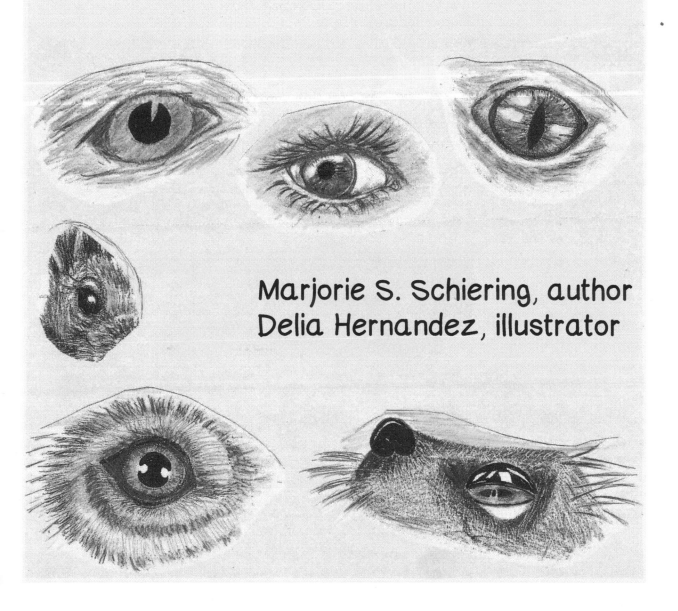

Marjorie S. Schiering, author
Delia Hernandez, illustrator

ISBN: 9781652226406

Ars Omnia Press

Visit our website at:
www.sophiaomni.org

Book Notes for Parents and Teachers
By: Dr. Marjorie S. Schiering

Welcome to the reading of *Whose Eyes Are These* and the enjoyment of the text, as well as the poems and accompanying hand-drawn animal pictures on each page. What follows are some suggestions for you, if you're reading this book to someone other than yourself:

1. Be aware that this book is an interactive/play-the-pages, rhyming, learning-from-context-clues, and coloring book that develops children's thinking skills;

2. Notice that on each page there is a missing word at the end of a poem's second stanza. This is where the child says or fills-in the word;

3. Realize that reading this book aloud to someone gives that person a chance to see if they're able to guess what animal's name completes the rhyme, and

4. Please help book listeners do that, or use the following methodologies for identifying the missing word (animal's name) by:

    a. Matching the rhyme,

    b. Using context clues that describe the animal, and/or

    c. Looking at the poem's accompanying picture of the animal.

Two Challenges:

- **Animal-name Challenge**: Use a piece of blank paper to cover the animal picture. See if the one listening to you read can use "a" and "b" above to determine the name of the animal that completes the rhyme.

- **Teaching-of-Thinking Challenge**: This is for identifying specific thinking skills used in the story. An example would be: When is the skill of "realizing" used and where is this seen or heard in the story?

For more information on this teaching-of-thinking, please consult my website: www.creativecognition4U.com

Book Notes for Children

Dear book-readers and page-players,

This is an interactive book where you are to fill-in the blank at the end of the poem on each page. That filling-in with writing or saying the animal's name is how you "play-the-page." These poems make a word-picture to help you name the animal to complete the poem's rhyme.

      Sometimes you may know the missing word. Sometimes you may not be sure of the missing word. But you can use: 1. The picture clue or 2. The rhyme to help you get the correct word for the empty space at the end of the poem.

      We encourage you to enjoy playing-the-pages of this picture book! And, if you have a few moments, it's suggested that you color the animal pictures by using crayons, pencils, or markers.

Warmly, Author: Marjorie
Illustrator: Delia

P.S. Enjoy the read, and when you're done, share this book with friends for fun!

"Whose eyes are these?" I wonder.
I really want to know.
I've seen them here and there,
Wherever I may go.

Sometimes they're large and wide,
Sometimes they're small and closed.
"Whose eyes are these?" I wonder.
"Just above one's nose."

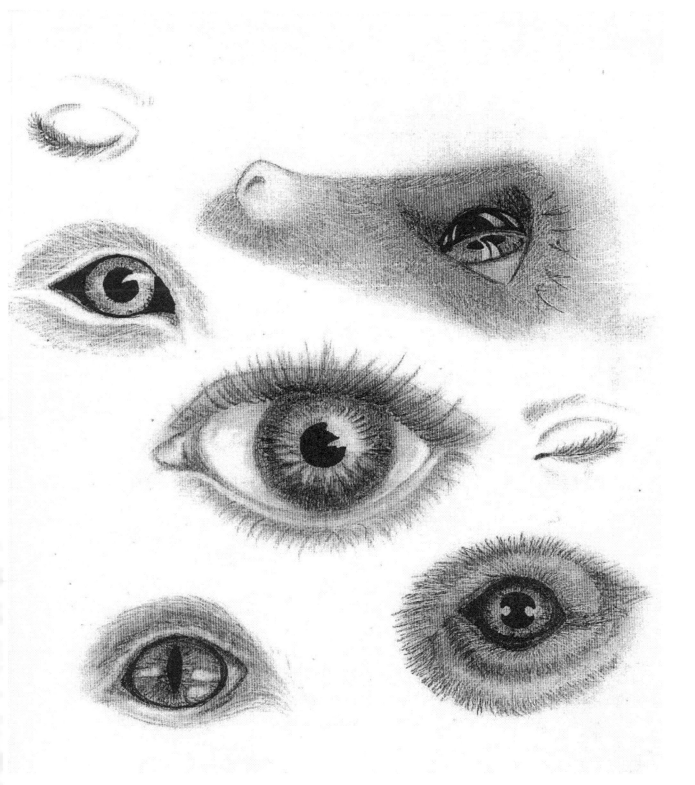

One day I got to thinking
About so many different eyes.
And, I asked myself how many
Could I identify?

So, I went outside my place.
Some eyes were by a log.
There, lying, sniffing flowers,
was our cute puppy _____ .

Next, I went around the corner,

and saw something flying there.

It was round and fuzzy,

moving without care.

And then, it started buzzing.

Its eyes were big, you see.

I guess I knew right then

It was a Honey _____ .

I walked over to the hillside

and started climbing slow.

I wondered what I'd see,

like . . . anything I know?

Then, something looked my way

Its eyes were big right now.

When it went: Moo, Moo, Moo,

I said, "This is a _____ ."

Just a few feet below,

on the very same hillside,

was a beautiful animal that,

I had once been on to ride.

It started walking my way.

I recognized it, of course.

With its eyes, long mane, and tail,

I knew it was a _____ .

It walked away from me,

as I looked into the sky.

The things that I saw next

went whooshing, flying by.

One landed on the ground.

Its name, I knew the word.

With beady eyes and feathers,

I knew this was a _____ .

Still outside my nice house

I saw a big brown chest.

It made a perfect seat

Where I sat down to rest.

Then, I got up quite quickly

I walked this way and that.

Two eyes were staring forward,

and were on my purring _____ .

Next, I walked around a while.

The weather was rather nice.

But suddenly it began to rain,

tiny droplets, the size of rice.

I decided then to go inside;

I heard a little splash-splish.

Several eyes stared up at me;

I was looking at my _____ .

Now, over to the window

I looked through the pane.

I saw eyes of an animal,

of which I knew the name.

This animal looked at me,

Its long ears rather funny.

It wiggled its soft nose.

Yes, it was a _____ .

And those are all the eyes

I saw this very day,

Inside my house and outside,

In the springtime month of _____ .

I thought this book had ended.

But it certainly has not,

Because some other sets of eyes

Are what this story's got.

As I stood there quietly thinking

I realized that I knew

There are many different eyes

That are on me and _____ .

Alternative Ending for which you will need a mirror

Then, I suddenly turned around,

And, I was surprised to see,

my image in the mirror.

Oh, these eyes belong to _____ .

29

CONGRATULATIONS!

You have completed playing-the-pages of this book by filling-in the missing animal's name!

We are proud of you!

Marjorie Schiering   and   *Delia Hernandez*

Author   Illustrator

Made in the USA
Middletown, DE
17 January 2021

31526253R00021